Absolute Pressure

orca sports

Sigmund Brouwer

Absolute Pressure

ORCA BOOK PUBLISHERS

Copyright © 2009 Sigmund Brouwer

All rights reserved. No part of this publication may be reproduced or transmitted in any form or by any means, electronic or mechanical, including photocopying, recording or by any information storage and retrieval system now known or to be invented, without permission in writing from the publisher.

Library and Archives Canada Cataloguing in Publication

Brouwer, Sigmund, 1959-
Absolute pressure / written by Sigmund Brouwer.
(Orca sports)
ISBN 978-1-55469-130-2 (pbk.)—ISBN 978-1-55469-164-7 (bound)

I. Title. II. Series.
PS8553.R68467A62 2009   jC813'.54   C2008-907422-x

First published in the United States, 2009
Library of Congress Control Number: 2008941145

Summary: Ian loves scuba diving and working in his uncle's dive shop in Key West, Florida. At least until someone tries to kill him—twice.

Mixed Sources
Cert no. SW-COC-001271
© 1996 FSC
FSC

Orca Book Publishers is dedicated to preserving the environment and has printed this book on paper certified by the Forest Stewardship Council.

Orca Book Publishers gratefully acknowledges the support for its publishing programs provided by the following agencies: the Government of Canada through the Canada Book Fund and the Canada Council for the Arts, and the Province of British Columbia through the BC Arts Council and the Book Publishing Tax Credit.

Cover design by Teresa Bubela
Cover photography by Getty Images
Author photo by Bill Bisley

ORCA BOOK PUBLISHERS   ORCA BOOK PUBLISHERS
PO Box 5626, Stn. B   PO Box 468
Victoria, BC Canada   Custer, WA USA
V8R 6S4   98240-0468

www.orcabook.com
Printed and bound in Canada.

13 12 11 10 • 5 4 3 2

To Jason Oakes with thanks
for all your help and encouragement.
Enjoy those Key West sunsets!

chapter one

One hundred and thirty feet doesn't sound like much. If you're walking.

You'd think twice if you were climbing that far. It's about twelve stories high. Nothing fun about clinging to the side of a building one hundred and thirty feet off the ground.

But what about the other direction? Underground or in shark-infested water.

In your mind, turn that twelve-story building upside down. Picture how far underwater the tip of the building would reach. Then think of going the entire distance straight down, where every cubic foot of water above you weighs over sixty pounds.

That's where I was headed at ten o'clock on a hot Thursday morning in August. Diving to a shipwreck, buried twelve stories under-water. It felt like the weight of the water was squeezing the light out of the sky. It was getting darker and darker by the second.

I was six miles offshore in the warm ocean water south of Key West in Florida. I had already swum twenty feet down. There was a thin nylon line on my weight belt. It was snapped to a thicker cable that dropped from the boat above. The thick line ended in a heavy anchor. Being hooked to this line made it easy to go straight down in the Gulf Stream.

Normally, I wouldn't use a guideline. I'd drift down from farther back and let the stream just take me. But this was a work dive, not a fun dive.

At thirty feet deep, I tilted my head to look up at the surface. The shadow of the *GypSea*—my uncle's dive boat—was a long black shape, like a fat cigar floating above me.

Far below me was another boat. This one, though, was much larger than the *GypSea*. It was also in much worse shape, since shipwrecks don't float or move very fast.

The shipwreck was an old US Air Force missile-tracking ship. It was almost the length of two football fields. There was no cool story about it sinking in a storm or anything like that. The ship had been cleaned up and then sunk on purpose. It was done to make a reef, a nice hiding place for fish and other undersea animals. It was also done so that tourists could scuba dive and explore it.

Tourists were part of my job. In fact, I was diving down to the wreck so I could hide a toy treasure chest for them. It was my idea. Business had not been good for a while. More people would hire my uncle's boat for dives, I thought, if we set up a treasure hunt for them.

The toy treasure chest I carried was not much bigger than a football. Inside it was a hundred-dollar bill wrapped in plastic to make it waterproof. The first diver to find it would keep the money.

I kicked my fins and swam down another ten feet. Slowly.

I don't like to hurry when I scuba dive. I also check and double-check everything. All the time. There is a saying in this sport: *There are old divers and there are bold divers, but there are no old bold divers.* In other words, not only can mistakes kill you, chances are they *will* kill you.

I dropped another ten feet. I was down to fifty feet. I had reached the top of the sunken ship. Fingers of steel reached up for me like a skeleton.

I stopped and hit a button to pump some air from my tank into special pockets built into my vest. I did this because as you go deeper, the weight of the water makes it harder to swim. By adding air to my vest, I was able to make myself lighter.

As I swam, I turned my head and watched for sharks. Especially hammerheads. Around Key West, they can be as long as a car. But much more dangerous. Cars just need gasoline for fuel. Sharks need meat and blood. Even though attacks are rare, I didn't want to be a quick fill-up for a shark.

I saw no sharks. There were plenty of smaller fish. Although I knew they were very colorful, they all looked bluish gray. Even clear water soaks up colors. After fifty feet, reds and oranges and yellows are gone. The blues disappear after sixty feet.

I only know the colors go away because that's what other people tell me. In my own little weird world, colors stay with me every-where. For instance, for me, Wednesdays are light blue. And whenever I hear the national anthem, I taste chocolate. Some people with my condition taste chocolate when they hear a Beethoven violin concerto. Some will hear a certain sound and get a tickling feeling. Or they'll feel something tickle them and hear a certain sound.

It's called *synesthesia*. When two senses are linked together. I know that sounds weird. That's why nobody knows I have it. Not even my mom. I don't want anyone to know I'm a freak.

At seventy feet deep, I still had another sixty feet to go to get to the bottom of the ship. There were elevator shafts and chambers and rooms long since stripped of equipment.

I checked the dial on my air tank. It showed full. I had only been in the water for fifteen minutes. Above me, in the *GypSea*, a guy named Judd Warner was waiting for me to return. He had just been hired by my uncle a couple of weeks earlier. Judd expected me back in half an hour.

I slipped inside the structure and kept going lower.

At eighty feet, I stopped to plug my nose through my dive mask. I swallowed hard and popped my ears, something I had been doing all the way down. It helps keep your eardrums from exploding.

At 130 feet, I finally found a great cubby hole deep inside the immense steel structure to hide the treasure chest in, and I began to rise again.

As I was going out of the cubby hole, a small fish brushed against my left elbow. Bright red filled my vision. I didn't panic. I knew about that spot on my elbow. Behind my right knee, there's a patch of skin that makes me see green whenever I rub it.

Yeah. Like I said, weird. But I've learned to live with it.

And I liked being alive.

Which was why I was always so careful when I went diving.

So what happened fifteen minutes later on my way up was a total shock.

At ninety-three feet, still inside the ship, something ripped my mouthpiece away from my face. And the water around me exploded.

chapter two

For a couple of seconds, I bucked and danced at the end of my line. I was like a rag doll shaken by a giant.

Was it a great white shark, twisting and turning me from side to side, like a bulldog with a rat in its jaws?

I couldn't see what was happening. It was dark, and air bubbles kept exploding around my face mask.

Don't panic! I told myself. *Don't panic!*

I tried to think it through. I didn't feel razor-sharp teeth cutting through my wet suit. So it wasn't a shark.

Don't panic. Don't panic.

I was still attached to the main cable that was my guideline. Without it, the force of the exploding water would have fired me in different directions like a pinball bouncing off flippers. If that had happened inside this ship, I'd already have broken arms or legs.

Don't panic. Don't panic.

With both hands, I grabbed for my mouthpiece. The rubber tube was like a live snake. It twisted and turned in the water, trying to get away from me.

I finally figured it out.

A pressure valve must have broken. Air in tanks is pressurized at about 3,000 pounds per square inch. A valve lets the air out slowly when you breathe. With a valve broken, this air was shooting out from the tank through the mouthpiece. In a hurry.

I was losing so much air and losing it so hard that the force of it was shaking my entire body.

I finally got my hands around the mouthpiece tube. I pulled the mouthpiece toward me.

I needed air!

There was no way I could get the mouthpiece back into place. The air was shooting out too hard. It would have been like turning on a garden hose and putting the end into my mouth and holding all the water. And trying to breathe air from the exploding bubbles would have been like trying to sip water from a fire hose.

My lungs screamed for air. But all I'd gulp into my lungs would be water.

With ninety-three feet to get to the surface.

chapter three

I tried to stay calm. In scuba diving, if you stop thinking, you're in trouble.

I knew I had two problems. One problem, of course, was needing air. There was lots of it above the water. But I'd have to swim that ninety-three feet straight up to get to it.

If you didn't know much about diving, you'd think that shouldn't be a problem. Just kick upward. A person should be able to hold his breath for a minute or two if he or she was in good shape.

A person could swim ninety-three feet in that time, right? That's only the distance from home plate to first base.

Except, like a lot of things in diving, it's more complicated that that.

If I didn't do it right, my lungs would explode. There was a simple reason for that. Absolute pressure. The combined total of atmospheric pressure and water pressure. The deeper you go, the more the weight of both squeezed things. Including air.

Once, out at sea, my Uncle Gordon had shown me exactly how it worked. He grabbed an empty plastic milk jug and took it with us to thirty-three feet underwater. He held the jug upside down, filled it with air from his scuba tank and capped the jug. He tied a rope around the handle of the jug and let it float up, like a balloon on a string.

I followed him as we slowly swam deeper and deeper. The pressure of the water squeezed the jug. It looked like an invisible hand was crushing it. At sixty-six feet, absolute pressure squeezed the jug to half the size it had been.

Because it was important that I understand, on the same day with the same milk jug, Uncle Gord had shown me how it worked in reverse. I'd never forgotten the lesson and what happened next.

At sixty-six feet, he added air to the crushed jug from his scuba tank. The pressurized air filled it until it was normal-sized again.

Uncle Gordon and I then swam back up, following the jug as it got closer and closer to the surface. As we got higher, the air in the jug pushed out because there was less water pressure squeezing it. It was like watching someone blow up a balloon. At thirty-three feet, the air inside expanded so much that the plastic jug ripped wide open.

My lungs were made of soft flesh. Not tough plastic like a milk jug. My lungs would become a mess of blood and pulp if I swam up too quickly. Fifty feet above me, with less pressure on me than at ninety feet, the air now inside my lungs would take up double the space. My lungs would explode.

Worse, when my lungs ripped inside me, air bubbles would get into my blood. And once those bubbles reached my brain, I'd be dead.

Ninety-three feet from the top and running out of air, there was only one thing to do. A thousand to one shot. Or even less of a chance than that.

I unsnapped myself from the guideline. I dropped the weights from my belt and kicked upward. Already I wanted to suck for air. But I forced myself to breathe out instead. I had to keep bleeding air out of my lungs so that they wouldn't explode like the plastic milk jug.

I kicked more. It got easier once I left the ship. Without the weights, I was like a cork. There was air in my diving vest too. That buoyant air was taking me higher and faster.

I kept pushing air out of my lungs. My body screamed for me to suck something in, not force it out. My body wanted to keep all the air. But if I held my breath, my lungs would rip.

Higher and higher. Second after second. I kept breathing out, kept pushing air out of my starving lungs.

Bam!

I felt something punch my chest. It was an air pocket in the vest, blowing apart as the air inside it expanded. It reminded me to keep pushing air out of my lungs, no matter what.

My sight became fuzzy and black around the edges. I needed air so badly I was about to pass out. But if I did, my body would try to breathe. My lungs would suck in water, not air.

The water grew brighter and brighter. But would I make the surface in time?

Then I remembered.

The boat!

If I was going straight up, I would hit the boat. Like a cork popping out of water. But corks don't have skulls that can be smashed. I did.

With my last ounce of energy, I kicked, trying to move straight ahead as I rose. I kicked. Kicked. Kicked...

The black around the edges of my eyesight expanded. I heard roaring in my ears. And finally, I hit sweet air.

My body popped all the way out of the water. When I landed, I saw the outline of the boat. Only ten feet away.

I sucked in lungful after lungful of air. Nothing in my life had ever felt better.

It had been close. Too close.

I waited for some energy to return. I swam toward the boat.

Judd leaned over. His face showed worry.

"Ian? Ian? What's the matter?"

I waved at him. It was a weak wave. I didn't have the strength for anything else. Not even the strength to talk.

I bumped up against the ladder. I tried to climb, but I couldn't. Judd reached down and helped me out of the water.

I got onto the boat.

"What happened?" Judd asked.

I groaned.

Water drained from my wet suit and my gear. I unbuckled my tank and vest and let both fall to the deck of the boat. I limped toward a bench seat. I let myself down. I lay back, staring at the blue sky.

And I waited to see if I would die.

chapter four

As I waited, I closed my eyes against the hot Florida sun. Seagulls, thinking we were a fishing boat, screamed as they flew in circles above us.

"Ian?" Judd said. "Talk to me, man."

"I'm scared I came up too fast." My throat was sore from sucking in air.

"What!" His voice told me he knew my fear. "But why?"

He didn't say the rest. He didn't say that only a stupid diver would come up fast.

"I think the valve went on my tank. My tank was blowing air. I had nothing to breathe."

"You made an emergency rise?"

"Yup." I groaned again. "No choice."

"How fast?"

"It happened at ninety-three feet. I went up on one last lungful of air."

"Straight up? Full speed?"

"You saw me pop out of the water."

"That's not good," he said. "How do you feel?"

"I don't know." I tried to smile. "Yet."

He knew how serious this was. He didn't need me to explain that I was wondering when the agony would hit me and curl me over into a whimpering ball.

He stepped past me and started the boat engines. Judd Warner was big. At six foot one, he had an inch of height on me and about twenty pounds. I'm seventeen. He was about ten years older. His hair was bleached blond by the sun and stringy from hours and hours in salt water. He wore shorts and a loose muscle shirt and moved with the smooth lightness of a cat.

"We're heading in," he said. "We've got to get you to a chamber."

I wouldn't have argued with him. Even if I'd had the energy.

Judd put both boat motors at full speed. We bounced across the green-blue water at forty miles per hour.

I tried not to think about what could happen if we didn't get there in time.

"I'm sorry, man!" Judd shouted as we cut across open water. The wind blew his hair straight back. "It should have been me down there!"

What he meant was that he should have been the one taking the treasure chest down to the wreck. But I loved diving. It was my life. I'd asked him a dozen times to let me go down until he'd gotten tired of arguing.

"That's okay," I said. "Remember? It was my idea to switch."

I don't think he heard me. I was too weak to shout above the wind.

Yeah. Diving was my life. Except now, even as I took air in through my lungs, it could be my death.

As we got closer to shore, I wondered if Judd was thinking what I was thinking. Things like broken valves don't happen to scuba diving tanks by accident.

If it wasn't an accident, that left two questions. Who had wrecked the valve? And why?

chapter five

There were two places Judd could take me in the Keys for a recompression chamber. One was in the upper Keys. The other was owned by the US military, right in Key West.

The military chamber was closer, and we were onshore in less than fifteen minutes.

Judd had radioed ahead, and an ambulance was waiting for me. Along with Uncle Gord and the girl who handled phone calls and did bookkeeping for the dive shop part-time.

Sherri Eaton.

As Judd banged the boat into the rubber dock bumpers, Uncle Gord and Sherri jumped down to where I was laying with my head on a towel, still in my wet suit.

Sherri Eaton was my age. Her mom was a neighbor of Uncle Gord's, and she'd been hanging around his dive shop every summer since I'd first started visiting Key West when I was ten years old.

As usual when Sherri was around, I hardly noticed Uncle Gord. First, she's tall and she's blond, and when she wears a swim suit, fire trucks and police cars could be racing each other in circles, and no one would notice anything except Sherri. And when she smiles, the sun has to take second place too.

I know I'm not the only guy who stutters when she's around.

But I'm guessing there's nobody else in the world who tastes blackberries when he sees her.

Yes. Blackberries. Much as I didn't like feeling like a freak, I guess there were some good things about synesthesia. She was beautiful, and I liked the taste of blackberries. It was a nice combination.

Not that I'd ever let her know about it. I wanted her to like me, not run away from me.

She leaned over, frowning with worry.

I was just as worried, wondering when the pain would hit, wondering if I would die, but even with all that worry, my tongue sent the taste of blackberries to my brain. Just for a few seconds.

"How are you feeling?" she asked.

Uncle Gord pushed her away. "What happened?"

He made me feel like a kid. I've been a certified diver for years, but he was almost a legend around Key West. I wanted to apologize, even though I hadn't done anything wrong.

"Broken valve," Judd answered for me. He pointed at the tank. "It's amazing he made it to the surface."

"What?" Uncle Gord's tanned face became a few shades darker. He's my mother's brother. They both had quick

tempers. But they were also quick to laugh.
I thought the world of both of them.
"An emergency rise?"

"Ninety-three feet," Judd said.

Sherri had moved in closer again. She
touched my elbow as she knelt beside me.
My left elbow. Bright red flooded my vision.
When it went away a few seconds later,
I saw that she was still beside me.

"Ninety-three feet?" She frowned again.
"Ian, tell me you're okay."

I didn't have time to answer. The ambulance crew was on the boat. With a stretcher
to take me to the decompression chamber.

"Sherri," I said. My voice was a croak.

She leaned in. Sherri always smelled
faintly of coconut oil. It was my favorite
smell. For a while I had wondered if that
smell was part of synesthesia too. Like the
taste of blackberries. Until I'd seen her use
some from a bottle.

"Ian?"

I couldn't imagine how nice it would
have been if she would have leaned a little
closer.

I was thinking that I might die. That I might never have a chance to tell her how I really felt about her. How much I wished just once she'd lean close enough to hug me.

"I really, really love blackberries," I said. If I was going to die, I wanted her to know how much I liked her. But before I told her how much I liked her, I'd have to work up the courage to tell her about my synesthesia.

"Ian?"

"Blackberries. Because when you—"

I couldn't finish my sentence. Bubbles in my blood hit me so hard that I bit through my tongue. There was the copper taste of blood and the warmth of it on my lips as it spilled from my mouth.

But that pain of my pierced tongue was nothing compared to getting hit by the bends.

I put my mouth into the crook of my arm and muffled my scream.

chapter six

Divers call it "the bends." They call it that because when you get it, you are forced to bend over with pain. It is a horrible pain. It hits the joints of elbows, shoulders and legs. If it's bad enough, it can make you blind or kill you.

Uncle Gord had explained the bends to me by telling me to think of a bottle of soda. Shake it hard and quickly open the cap. Watch it bubble over. Then think of bubbles popping out of your blood in the same way. Major pain.

It has to do with the same water pressure that squeezed the milk jug.

You see, the normal air that you breathe every day has nitrogen in it, along with oxygen. Scuba diving tanks have the same mixture. As you breathe underwater, the pressure of the water's weight on your body slowly forces the nitrogen gas into your blood. The longer you stay down, the more nitrogen is in your blood.

It's not a problem, as long as you make sure the nitrogen gas leaves just as slowly as it went in. Just like with a plastic bottle of soda. If you open the cap a little at a time, the pressure is released slowly. The soda doesn't fizz. But if you go up too fast in diving, you take the pressure off too fast. You become like a bottle of soda with the cap popped off. The pressure lets go all at once, and the gasses inside the soda make bubbles and fizz over. Except in diving, the bubbles fizz in your blood. That's bad news.

It was the same bad news for me. Instead of going up at the ideal rate of fifteen feet per minute, I had shot upward like a cork. Nitrogen bubbles were already forming in my blood.

Now, curled up in an ambulance that was racing down the streets with sirens on and lights flashing, my only hope was the recompression chamber at the end of the ride.

On the outside, a recompression chamber looks like a mini-submarine, with gauges everywhere. Inside, it can seat up to three divers.

At the military base, they rushed me inside.

I did my best not to scream at the pain as they moved me toward the recompression chamber.

They closed it on both ends, and began to pump air into it. The air wouldn't escape and it would put pressure on my body. Just like putting a cap on the top of a bottle of soda to stop the fizzing.

As long as it wasn't too late.

chapter seven

I had about seven hours ahead in the recompression chamber. If I was lucky and survived.

The pressure in the chamber rose to about two atmospheres. That's double the pressure you feel standing outside.

Actually, you don't feel the pressure. You have just as much pressure inside you pushing out as you have air pressing down on you. That may sound confusing, but it's like this.

When you are on a beach, the entire weight of all the air above is pressing down on you. Sure, air doesn't weigh a lot. But when there is sixty miles of it pressing down on you, it adds up.

In fact, it could crush you.

The reason it doesn't is because it also fills you and pushes out.

Still doesn't make sense?

Suck the air out of a plastic soda bottle and watch what happens. It crumples. The only reason it normally holds its shape is because the atmosphere is pushing air *into* it at the same time it is pushing air *onto* it.

In the recompression chamber, the pressure against me was countered by the pressure inside me as the air filled my lungs. At the same time, it was stopping nitrogen bubbles from fizzing inside my blood.

"How's it feel?" The voice came from a doctor outside the chamber, through a speaker inside.

"Better," I said. "Much better."

I was able to sit up as the pain eased.

"You're a certified diver," the doctor said. "Right?"

"Right."

"So you know what to expect."

"Right."

But he told me anyway. "In a few hours, we'll bring you up to thirty feet."

What he meant was that right now, my body was under the same pressure as it would be if I were sixty feet underwater. I was slowly getting rid of the nitrogen that had been forced into my blood by pressure. After some of it was gone, the pressure would be reduced.

"I think you'll be fine," he said. "We'll keep you monitored. In the meantime, there's lots of stuff to read in there."

I nodded. I didn't mind reading. I'd long gotten used to seeing every *M* in purple and every *S* in orange. It's just the way I was. For a long time, when I was in elementary school, I thought everybody saw the alphabet the same way.

Once I learned differently though, it wasn't something I ever talked about. People already felt sorry enough for me because of my dad.

You see, in the middle of my kindergarten year, he died.

Or, at least, everyone thought he was dead.

We lived in Chicago. Near the lake. He went sailing in his small boat one day and disappeared in a storm. The boat was found, and his life jacket washed up onshore. But no sign of him.

My mom almost went crazy, she was so sad. Me too, but I didn't really understand what had happened. All I can remember was that I'd fall asleep crying every night because my daddy had not come home. When he was finally declared legally dead, she cried for another couple of months. Me too.

A few years later, someone from the life insurance company stopped by the house. He asked if my mom knew that my dad was still alive. And asked her what she had done with the life insurance money.

She said it wasn't true. And that she hadn't collected any money.

Then they showed her a photo of my dad with another woman. He was married to someone else. He had a different name. I never saw him again, but I learned to hate him anyway. I was glad he went to jail, but I never visited him.

It turned out that he had faked his death and found a way to intercept the life insurance that should have been going into their joint account. After that, Mom really changed. Sad. Quiet. Never talked to people. Hardly even to me. It was like she was going through the motions of living.

She sent me to Key West every summer. It's almost like Uncle Gord raised me instead of her. Except Uncle Gord was more like an army sergeant than a father. I sure wasn't going to tell him how weird I was. Tasting blackberries when I saw Sherri. Seeing bright red when something touched my left elbow. Stuff like that.

So I just concentrated on what I loved best. Diving.

Absolute Pressure

As I sat in the recompression chamber, I wondered when I'd be able to dive next. Because if the broken valve wasn't an accident, what would happen next?

chapter eight

The next morning, I was in the back room of Uncle Gord's dive shop. Not dead. Not blind. Not bent over in pain. I had spent seven hours in the chamber, and the doctors had sent me on my way.

"Your guess was right, Ian," Uncle Gord said. "The broken valve wasn't an accident."

Like my mother, Uncle Gord has hair that turned gray early. He has a bushy mustache that is still as dark as the rest of his hair used to be. Like my mother, he's not real big. But he's in great shape from diving all the time. He's in his forties, but I doubt many people would want to mess with him in a fight.

"Look at this," he said.

Gord's Dive Shop has four rooms. There is the sales floor with scuba diving gear. Masks. Flippers. Wet suits. Spearguns. Tanks. Books on the sport. Everything.

On one side is a doorway leading to a long and narrow room. This is the training room. It has a long table where up to twelve people can sit. At the front end is a chalk board. Uncle Gord uses this room when he gives dry-land lessons on scuba diving.

There is also a back room with a work bench. It's where we fill the scuba diving tanks with air and do repairs.

The fourth room is Uncle Gord's office. It is tiny. Hardly larger than his messy desk. He always keeps the door locked so that customers don't wander in.

He was standing at the work bench. Tools were scattered across the top of it.

The valve parts of my scuba tank were in front of him.

I moved beside him to look at the tank.

"See," he said, pointing. "Look at where the spring broke apart."

The spring was from the valve. It was strong enough to keep the valve partly closed against the air pressure inside the tank. Except it had broken into two pieces.

"Yes?" I wasn't sure what he meant.

"Use the magnifying glass."

I did. As I looked at it up close, he kept talking.

"It's like a tree you cut with a saw," he said. Uncle Gord loved using examples. "The cut is smooth most of the way through. But when the tree falls, the last little bit breaks away and leaves a jagged edge."

He was right. On one side of the broken spring, it was shiny, as if it had been snipped halfway through. The other side was jagged, like it had been ripped apart.

"I don't get it," I said.

"I do," he told me. He frowned. "And I don't like it."

I waited.

"You know all about water pressure," he said.

I nodded yes. It had just about killed me the day earlier.

"Someone took this valve apart and cut most of the way through the spring. Then he put it back together. The spring was still strong enough to hold in shallow water. But in deeper water, it would only be a matter of time until the pressure blew it apart."

"In other words," I said, "someone wanted this accident to happen in deep water."

"Exactly. What if you had been deep inside the shipwreck when this happened instead of near the opening?"

I gulped. Sometimes it takes ten minutes just to swim out of a wreck.

"I'd be dead," I told him.

Uncle Gord stared at me for nearly a minute. He has light blue eyes. They didn't blink as he thought about it.

"I already know a lot of the story," he finally said. "You dove instead of Judd."

"Yes, sir," I said.

"Even though I had told you I wanted you on the surface in the boat."

"I've dived lots," I said. "I'm certified. You taught me to be careful. I didn't think you'd mind."

"What I mind is him not doing what I paid him for. He was supposed to go down into the wreck. Not you."

"Yes, sir."

Uncle Gord stared at me for another minute. I remembered some stories I'd heard about him getting into fights when he was younger. I'd heard he was tougher than most guys twice his size. By the cold look in his eyes, I was able to believe it.

"Tell me," he said. "Did you ask Judd if you could make the dive? Or did he ask you?"

My body suddenly felt as cold as Uncle Gord's eyes. I understood his question. If Judd had asked me to go down, maybe he knew about the valve and that it would bust in deep water.

"I asked to dive," I said. "Honest. It was my idea. I was bored and wanted something to do. It was my fault this happened."

Uncle Gord slammed the work bench so hard that a wrench jumped and fell to the floor.

"It wasn't your fault," he said, his face angry. "It was the fault of whoever wrecked the valve spring."

He hit the table again. "I'm going to find out who did this."

Uncle Gord took a deep breath. He waited until he was calm.

"Ian," he said, "you and I are going to keep this a secret. That way, the person who did it won't know we're looking for him."

"What about the police?" I asked. "Shouldn't they know?"

Uncle Gord put his hands on my shoulders. He looked right into my eyes. "You know that business has not been great this year. What's going happen if people hear about this? They'll think we don't run safe dives. They might not buy equipment from us."

"But—"

"No buts. I think I know why someone would have done this," he said. "I'm going to tell you another secret. It's the real reason why I take the dive boat out on Friday and Saturday nights."

I asked Uncle Gord a simple question. "Does any of this have anything to do with a sunken pirate ship and a ton of gold?"

chapter nine

Uncle Gord's square jaw fell. For a second, with his eyes bugged out and his jaw open wide, he looked like a fish just pulled from water.

"How did you know about that?" he said.

"I don't think it's much of a secret," I said. "This is a small town."

"Tell me what you know. Tell me *how* you know."

I shrugged. "I heard the rumor two weeks ago. When I was with Judd. We were at the dock, putting gas in the dive boat. One of the guys there asked me if it was true you were looking for a pirate ship."

"And?" Uncle Gord seemed worried.

"I told the guy I didn't know. Which was true. But I've been wondering. Along with a lot of other people in town. Everyone knows you go out every week with those three lawyers from Miami. No one believes that you are just a spear-fishing guide."

They had hired Uncle Gord every weekend since the beginning of May. Each Friday and Saturday night, Uncle Gord left at sunset with the three of them and didn't return until dawn.

"Spear fishing is what we've wanted people to believe," Uncle Gord finally said. "But once you heard the rumors, why didn't you ask me about it?"

"It isn't my business," I said. "I figured you'd tell me if you ever wanted to."

Uncle Gord let out a deep breath. "I was afraid of this. That's why I don't like what happened to the valve on your scuba tank. If our secret is out, maybe someone wants to stop us."

"Will you tell me about it now?" I asked. "Is it really true what people are saying?"

He looked around, as if he were afraid someone might be listening. But there were no customers in the front or the back of the shop.

Sherri wasn't there either. I knew her schedule. She didn't work until the afternoon.

"Let's go down to the coffee shop," Uncle Gord said. "I'll tell you what I can."

chapter ten

We walked. Thelma's Diner was just down the road from the dive shop. It was late afternoon, and the sun was still strong and hot. When we got inside, Thelma came over to our table.

"What will it be, boys?" She had five kids and ran the diner by herself. She always looked tired.

"Same as always," Uncle Gord said. "A couple of iced teas. A couple of orders of fries."

"Sure." She wiped our table with a rag. A minute later she brought the iced tea. When she left, she went into the kitchen. There was no one else in the diner. Uncle Gord and I could talk and not worry that someone would hear.

"I'm waiting," I said.

Uncle Gord drank half his glass of iced tea before he spoke. "I'll make the story as short as I can. It started in the spring when the three lawyers came down here from Miami. They told me a story of their own."

I added sugar to my iced tea and stirred as I listened.

"A few years ago, some guy was scuba diving a couple of miles from here. He found some gold coins in water about thirty feet deep. They looked very old and valuable. He hired the law firm to find out more about the coins."

"Why a law firm?" I asked.

"Because lawyers have to keep client confidentiality. He knew if the lawyers talked, he could sue them. He also wanted to hire them to help him keep the rest of the treasure once he found it."

"It doesn't seem like the lawyers kept it much of a secret," I said.

"You're right. But the guy died just after hiring them. He didn't have a family or anything. No will. Once he died, these three lawyers figured they might as well look for the treasure themselves."

"Treasure," I said. "Real treasure. Not like the toy treasure I hid in the wreck for you yesterday."

"Real treasure. Big, big treasure. Because when the lawyers found out more about the coins..."

Uncle Gord leaned across the table. His voice became a whisper. "Ian, they had a professor look at the coins. They're from a Spanish ship that came here in the 1700s. It was delivering gold from the king of Spain. Pirates hit the ship and took everything. A week later, the pirate ship went down in a hurricane off the coast of Florida. The coins today would be worth over ten million dollars."

It took me a second to realize I was sucking air through my straw. I had been listening so closely, I had drunk all my iced tea without knowing it.

"You know this for sure?" I asked.

"For sure," he said. "The lawyers paid for careful research in libraries and museums. These coins were made for a special occasion. The birth of the king's daughter. They could have only come from one ship."

"But how did the guy find the coins when he was scuba diving? Didn't he find the ship too?"

"The last hurricane," he said.

"Huh?"

"You know, the biggest storm to hit Florida in two hundred years. These lawyers figure the storm moved some sand around in shallow water. The same sand that was covering the pirate ship. Their guess is that the storm caused the coins to spread out from the ship."

Uncle Gord took a paper napkin. With a pencil from his pants pocket, he began to draw the different islands around Key West. He also drew some arrows going south to north.

"Here's the Gulf Stream," he said, pointing at the arrows. "You know how strong it is."

I did. All divers did. The stream was caused by water heating in the south and flowing north toward the poles of the earth, where the water cooled again.

"These lawyers had weather scientists make charts," Uncle Gord continued. "The charts showed the currents and the storm movement of the hurricane. The charts showed how strong the current was during the storm and how fast it moved. From those charts and from where the coins were found, they tried to track how far the coins would have moved."

I became excited. "Because if they can track the coins, they can track them backward to where they came from."

Uncle Gord grinned. "Now you know why I agreed to help them. They have narrowed the search to an area twenty miles long and half a mile wide. Right where the Gulf Stream is the strongest."

His grin became a frown. "But twenty miles long and half a mile wide is still ten square miles. That's a lot of ocean floor to explore. The four of us have been doing it on weekends. We look around and mark off the area on our map so that we don't go back to it again. We figure it might take a year or two to search all of it."

Thelma was coming toward us with our French fries. I waited until she was gone before I said anything.

"That's why you wanted people to think you were spear fishing," I said. "You don't want anyone else looking for it."

Uncle Gord dipped one of the fries into ketchup. "Exactly," he said. "Night is a great time to do it. We have good lights for underwater, and fewer people can see us. But from what you said, it's not much of a secret anymore. And that's bad news for two reasons."

"Yes?"

"One, I have no idea how the secret got out. Maybe one of the three lawyers is trying a double cross."

"And the other reason?" I asked. Hungry as I was, I hadn't touched my fries yet.

"I don't know if you noticed," Uncle Gord said. "But the scuba tanks that you and Judd took out today? They're the tanks I usually use. I think someone wants *me* dead."

chapter eleven

I felt guilty when I left the diner to go to the library.

Not because the library is a bad place to be. Just the opposite. Much as I love Key West and the different kinds of people who call it home, sometimes Duval Street is a little crazy. The library is a few blocks off Duval. I love the quiet inside. I love getting lost inside books. I love how I can be alone, but not feel lonely.

I felt guilty because I was headed to the library to do some snooping. Without Uncle Gord knowing about it.

I headed down Duval, away from the harbor. I loved the buildings with second-story balconies hanging over the street. Buildings weathered by sun and storm and hurricanes were part of Key West. Just like the people who made Key West their home.

There were old people on motorized carts and guys with long beards and deep tans and no shirts. There were sunburned tourists gawking at the guys with long beards and no shirts. The streets in front of the bars were quiet because it was morning, but at night the streets would be lit up and magical with music and loud conversations. Sometimes I walked Duval at that time. Sometimes that too was a good place to be alone but not lonely.

I crossed Eaton Street. Which, as always, reminded me of Sherri Eaton. I knew her family had been here a long time. Someday, when I stopped stuttering around her, I'd ask if she was related to the Eaton that the street had been named after.

I reached the Empress, a store with cool-looking white balconies on the second floor, and turned left to go up Fleming Street to the library.

As usual, there were too many cars on the street. I wasn't the only one who complained about it. But with the smell of the trees and flowers and the sunshine on my shoulders, it still seemed like a great day.

Especially because the recompression chamber had saved me from any permanent damage like blindness.

Now all I had to worry about was who was trying to get rid of Uncle Gord.

Maybe I'd find my answers at the library. Same way I'd finally found why I tasted blackberries whenever I saw Sherri Eaton.

When someone like me doesn't want to talk to people about what's happening inside them, there's a way to ask around without talking to anyone.

The Internet. And Google.

With the air-conditioning drying the sweat at the center of my back, I googled on a library computer. I could have done it at Uncle Gord's house, but one of the great things about the library was that you could expand your research with their books. Plus, I lived with Uncle Gord. I didn't want him finding out what I was doing.

I learned about the kings of Spain in the 1700s. Philip V, Louis I, Ferdinand VI, Charles III and Charles IV. As usual, I ignored the purple *M*s and orange *S*s as I read about them.

There were pictures of each of the kings. In their long flowing costumes and fancy wigs and ornate jewelry, they could have walked down Duval some nights and no one would have looked twice.

I read about their daughters. I read about their ships. I read about their wars. I read about their gold coins.

I was careful in my search. I knew that Key West had not always been called Key West. This guy named Ponce de León discovered Florida for Spain in the 1500s. Legend says he was looking for the Fountain of Youth—water that would keep him from getting old. When Ponce and his sailors first saw the thick mangrove trees on the shores, with their twisted roots reaching into the water like human limbs, they called it *Los Mártires*. The Martyrs.

It took about a hundred years for Key West to show up on maps, but back then it wasn't Key West. It was called Cayo Hueso—Bone Key—because the first explorers discovered bones of Calusa Indians who'd been driven south from key to key until they could go no further. They fought their last battle on Key West, leaving their skeletons to bleach in the sun. Or so the story goes.

Pretty soon, people found it easier to say Key than Cayo, and West than Hueso. And Cayo Hueso was replaced by Key West.

And when I found what I was looking for, I whistled so loud in surprise that a couple of old ladies frowned at me from a nearby table.

I didn't care.

What I was reading was an Internet rumor on a treasure-hunting website. It described how a ship went down off Key West in a hurricane in 1748.

The article said that nothing had ever been confirmed about the shipwreck. Most people believed it didn't exist.

But now the lawyers had something to confirm this rumor: the gold coins their client had brought them in utmost secrecy.

Now I understood why the lawyers were trying to keep it secret.

If the treasure existed, it was supposed to be worth over three hundred million dollars.

That was the kind of money that people killed for.

And the kind of money that people died for too.

chapter twelve

I made it back to the dive shop just after lunch. Sherri was already there. I waited for the taste of blackberries. It came and went.

"Hey," she said. "Uncle Gord called me when you made it out of recompression last night. Sounds like everything is all right."

She was behind the front counter of the sales floor, at the computer.

"Yes," I answered. "No."

"Your eyes?" She looked worried. She knew as much about the bends as I did. "You can see okay, can't you?"

I could. And, looking at her face and shiny blond hair, I was glad I could.

"I'm okay," I said. I went to the back to see if Uncle Gord was around. There was the usual smell of mildew and sea salt on scuba diving equipment.

Uncle Gord wasn't there. I came back. I lowered my voice.

"Have you heard the rumors in town about Uncle Gord?" I asked.

"Pirate ships." She smiled.

"I heard that too," I said. I tried to act like it was no big deal. But it was a big deal. If other people knew that three hundred million dollars was involved, Uncle Gord could be in big trouble.

"I don't take it too seriously," she continued. "Lots of people around here want to believe in sunken treasure. Lots of people look. Lots of people think they are only one trip away from the big find. I mean, remember Mel Fisher?"

There was a museum in Key West, the Mel Fisher Maritime Museum. Although he wasn't alive any more, people sure remembered him. He searched the waters west of the Key for over twenty years, and finally found silver, gold and emeralds in a Spanish shipwreck named the *Atocha*. It was worth hundreds of millions of dollars.

"Say Uncle Gord was seriously looking. Say it wasn't a rumor."

"You mean every Friday night when he goes out with those guys and pretends to be fishing?"

"Yeah," I said. "Heard anything else about it?"

She was still smiling. "Why would you be worried?"

"Hey," I said, "what makes you think I'm worried?"

"When I asked if you were okay. You said yes and no. Yes, you're okay after yesterday's accident. So it must be something else." Another great smile. "Plus you look worried. You're not good at hiding things, you know."

I'd hidden what I felt about her. But I sure wasn't going to tell her that.

And much as I wanted to, I couldn't tell her about the busted valve on the air tank either. Maybe the lawyers from Miami were getting close to finally finding the treasure. Maybe they wanted to get rid of Uncle Gord so they wouldn't have to share it with him.

"I need a favor," I said. "It's about those Miami lawyers who book Uncle Gord every weekend."

She nodded.

"I only know their first names," I said. "Can you look up their last names?"

"Got it on the computer," she said. "Give me a second or two."

She rattled her fingertips across the keyboard, staring at the screen. Her fingertips didn't make much of a clicking sound. She kept her fingernails cut pretty short. I noticed these things about her.

"Here we go," she said. "Come around and look at this."

I looked at the computer. There wasn't much information. Just their names. John

The balloon hats were animal-shaped. She wore a giraffe. Blue. He wore a rabbit. Red.

One of the buskers here in Mallory Square, on the very west side of the Key, had made the hats for them. They probably paid him ten dollars for the balloons.

And they seemed happy about paying that much for a few balloons worth only a couple of pennies each.

See, tourists come here to be happy. To soak in the sun and the lifestyle where people don't care about suits and ties. Maybe Mr. Rabbit Balloon was a banker in a small town where everyone expected him to be serious all the time. Here, he could be himself.

Especially as sunset approached.

Every night, Key West had a sunset celebration. I loved it. As people relaxed and gathered at the edge of Mallory Square to watch the setting sun, they enjoyed street performances too. There were the buskers—people who performed for tips— like the balloon maker, a couple of jugglers, a tight-rope walker, a unicyclist with a trained dog, a sword swallower, some magicians and even a bagpiper.

Other people sold arts and crafts. Wood sculptures. Metal sculptures. Jewelry. T-shirts. Paintings.

And some were happy to turn anyone else into art. They painted on your body or gave cool hair wraps and braids. You could even get a body massage out there in the square.

It was festive and magical and noisy and fun. It was another one of my favorite places to be alone without feeling lonely.

Yet as much energy as the buskers and performers and tourists added to the square, it always lost to the majesty and beauty and peace of the sunset.

From Mallory Square, the view west across the flat water was amazing as the sun came closer and closer to the horizon. On clear nights, the sun was an orange glow that seemed to sink into the gulf. If there were clouds, the colors would be streaks of orange and red and purple.

And as the sun came closer and closer to the horizon, people would turn away from their amusements and get lost in something as pure and untouched as the rest of the universe. The sunset.

I'd get lost too. Most nights.

Except tonight.

I had ducked a juggler, avoided a tattoo salesman and dodged the unicylist when I saw Uncle Gord.

He was at the edge of the square. Facing away from the sunset. Between a couple of guys a couple of inches taller than him.

Normally, I wouldn't think twice. Uncle Gord loved Mallory Square too. He knew most of the performers and buskers because he'd been living here all his life. He'd walk around, talking, laughing.

But here, he was away from the crowds. As if the two bigger guys had dragged him away.

And Uncle Gord's shoulders were up near his ears. I hardly ever saw him like that. It was something he did when he was so angry his muscles bulged like he would explode. His powerful shoulders would rise and rise, and his elbows would go way back.

As I wondered if I should go over and help, Uncle Gord snapped his right fist forward and smashed one of the guys in the nose. It happened so fast, if I hadn't been watching, I would not have seen it.

chapter fifteen

No one else seemed to notice.

The guy he had hit bent over and clutched his nose.

That's when I began jogging. I only had about twenty-five steps to go. I didn't want to go so fast that it would draw attention.

The second guy had backed away so Uncle Gord couldn't hit him too. I got there just as the second guy pulled out a switchblade. He was holding it low, so that no one else in the crowd would notice.

I don't think it mattered. Everyone was looking at the sunset.

"Got your back," I said to Uncle Gord.

"Go away," he said without looking at me.

"Got your back," I repeated. I pulled out my best weapon. My cell phone. "If these guys try anything, I'll have it on video."

"The kid is dead," the second guy said.

"Ian, go away," Uncle Gord said. "This is my business."

"Can't," I said. "You guys going to run, or do I need to start shooting video? I can have it on the Internet in less than an hour. You'll be famous."

The second guy snapped some Spanish words at the first guy. They backed away. The first guy had blood streaming between his fingers. Uncle Gord had probably broken his nose.

When they got to the street, they began running. In seconds, they were out of sight.

"Thanks," Uncle Gord said. His face was red in the last rays of the sun. "I think."

"What was going on?" I asked.

"Just drop it," he said.

"You're my uncle," I said. "You've taken me in every summer. How can I drop it?"

"It would be the best thing you could do for me."

"It's about the treasure, isn't it?" I took a deep breath. "I know how much it's worth."

He stared at me for a long time. In the background, someone was playing the bagpipes.

"I wish you didn't know anything," he said.

"I want to help." Then I began to blurt it all out. "The Miami guys are lying to you. They are not Abbot and Gardner and Betz."

"What!"

I told him how I found out.

"Does anyone else know?"

I thought of Sherri. I didn't want her to get in trouble. She shouldn't have even told me about Judd. I couldn't let Uncle Gord know that I knew.

So instead of answering, I finished with a question. "You think if you're getting close to finding the treasure, they want you out of the way? Like maybe one of them made sure the valve on the tank would break?"

Uncle Gord's shoulders slumped now.

Finally, Uncle Gord sighed. "Thanks for telling me this, Ian. Give me a few days to figure out what to do, all right? That's all I'm asking. A few days."

"It's the treasure, isn't it?" I repeated.

"It's the treasure," he said. "And it's one big mess."

chapter sixteen

"Hey," Uncle Gord said, "let's shoot some underwater shark video."

It was morning. We were at Thelma's Diner. Uncle Gord was talking like it was just another day. I was happy to pretend it was too. If that made him feel better, I was all for it.

"Yeah," he continued. "We'll go down in the shark cage." He grinned. "But we'll make it exciting. We'll bring some hamburger in with us."

I knew what he meant. Our shark cage was ten feet by ten feet by ten feet. Made of aluminum bars spaced every six inches. A big square with an open top. There were floats all around the outside, about a quarter of the way down from the top. The floats held the cage upright, but allowed most of it to remain underwater. We lowered tourists into the center of the cage. The tourists had snorkels and masks. They could stand in the cage and duck their heads under the water to look at the sharks.

We brought the sharks in with meat. Bloody meat.

After the cage was lowered into the water, held to the boat by a towrope, we'd throw the meat into the water. It would bring sharks in from miles away. Little ones. Big ones. The most spectacular were the great white sharks, the tiger sharks and the bull sharks.

"Hamburger inside the cage?" I said.

"The video will show them bumping the bars trying to get in. We'll post it on our website. It will be a great marketing tool."

I liked the idea. The shark cage was safe. And if it would bring in more phone calls and e-mails from people who wanted to hire Uncle Gord and the *GypSea*, that was good. I knew he needed the business.

"I'm in," I said.

"Good."

"As long as you let me shoot the video," I continued.

"Why do you get all the fun?" he grinned.

"That mean I can do it?"

"Sure," he said. "What could go wrong?"

Famous last words.

chapter seventeen

Ten miles out of Key West, I stood on the deck of the *GypSea* and watched angry sharks bump at the cage in the blue Gulf waters.

Uncle Gord and I had chummed the waters to bring them in. We'd thrown out chopped up fish, knowing the scent of oily blood would bring sharks in from all directions.

We'd saved the raw hamburger for the center of the cage. Five pounds, in a mesh bag that kept it from dropping through the floor of the cage.

Now the sharks were banging at the cage, which was held in position by the floats three-quarters up the sides. Six, maybe seven, sharks. Just little ones. Three to five feet long. Nothing really exciting.

Then I saw a big, dark shadow. A big dark shadow that came to the surface.

I felt a tingle.

Not the kind of tingle when my senses get mixed up.

But the kind of tingle that said *danger*.

It was a bull shark.

A great white shark will shake you and spit you out. Bull sharks hold on and chew, like bulldogs but with a hundred times more teeth and strength. Bull sharks eat anything and everything. Fish, seals, turtles, smaller sharks. Even license plates or pieces of old tire. And whenever you read about a shark attack on a human, chances are it was a bull shark.

This big dark shadow wasn't just a bull shark though. The average bull shark is big enough—seven feet—and end to end will be longer than some couches.

This one was half as big again. A female. Its nose could touch one wall of an average room, and its tail would curl against the opposite wall. Fast, mean, unpredictable. The perfect killer. Some grew as big as eleven feet, seven hundred pounds.

"Uncle Gord," I whispered. I didn't need to whisper. But it was so scary I was afraid to draw its attention. I couldn't take my eyes off it. Like I was a rabbit, and it was a python hypnotizing me. "Check it out."

Uncle Gord moved beside me.

"Dang," he said, with admiration. "Can't ever remember seeing one that big. This is perfect."

The other sharks had scattered. In fear.

This monster nosed the cage. Its dorsal fin broke the surface of the water, showing a gleaming dark blue triangle. I shuddered at the thought of what it would be like to be treading water and see a fin like that approach.

The bull shark bumped the cage a little harder, trying to get at the mesh bag of hamburger inside. The cage bounced on its floats.

The shark turned away, but in a flash swirled back and hit the cage hard. Maybe it was my imagination, but the bars seemed to dent a little.

"Ready?" Uncle Gord said. "We've got to get footage of this before it gives up."

No. I wasn't ready.

It's one thing to talk about it over breakfast in a diner. Onshore. Safe.

It's another to be on a gently swaying deck of a boat in a hundred feet of water. Looking down at a monster shark that was angry and hungry and could take off an arm with a single swipe of its jaws.

But I'd said I would do it.

And the cage was perfectly safe. No shark would be able to break through the bars, because the cage was floating and would simply bounce away. The tops of the bars were more than a foot out of the water. The shark wouldn't be able to jump over top and get inside, even if its tiny brain figured out how to do it.

Although my emotions told me it was insane to get into the cage, my brain told me nothing could go wrong.

So I put on my snorkel and mask, grabbed the underwater camera and climbed down the ladder of the *GypSea* into the cage.

To face the monster.

chapter eighteen

I was in a wet suit.

I wished I were in chain mail.

All that the wet suit could do was protect me from the cold water. Even though Gulf waters are warm compared to other areas, the temperature is still lower than body temperature. It never hurts to stay warm.

The floor of the cage was about eight feet below the surface. It meant that I was treading water inside the cage, looking directly at the dorsal fin of the bull shark on the other side of the bars. I could have reached through and touched it.

The shark must have seen my legs and arms moving below the surface. It charged the cage again, sending shudders through the water.

I gulped and told myself again that the cage could take it.

Then I lowered my head and put my mask in the water and began to breathe through the snorkel.

I almost wet myself inside my wet suit.

With the mask showing everything underwater so clearly, I could see the shark's jaws opened wide enough to swallow a basketball. It was directly on the other side of the bars, angled sideways, trying to get through to me.

It was so terrifying, I almost forgot to turn on the underwater camera.

Bang. It hit the cage again.

Scary as this was, I knew it would make for some good footage.

Bang.

Bang.

As I concentrated on filming the shark as it swirled around and attacked the cage, I forgot to be afraid. My world was reduced to the shark and the water and the sound of my breathing.

Until I noticed something as terrifying as the shark.

One of the cage's outside floats had drifted away from the cage!

That side of the cage immediately began to sink.

Now the cage was tilting sideways. Before, there had been quite a bit of the cage above the water on all four sides. Now the side without the float had sunk below the surface.

And, unbelievably, another float drifted away from the cage.

Without warning, and before I could react, two sides of the cage were well underwater. The top of the cage was now three feet below the surface, with the open end of the cage beginning to face sideways.

With the shark coming in hard. Directly at me.

chapter nineteen

Strange how a person's mind can register things so clearly.

This close to the surface, there was plenty of sunlight. Behind the shark, I saw bright particles of plankton suspended in the water, like dust in a beam of light.

I saw the shark's blank eyes. I saw rows of sharp triangular teeth, all pointing inward. I even saw a few strands of meat stuck in those teeth, floating like streamers.

I had no way of protecting myself.

In the movies, the good guy will punch the shark on the nose and frighten it away.

That was the movies. Here it would have done as much good as spitting in the face of a grizzly.

The shark filled the entire opening of the cage. The cage that was now my prison.

And then, with the clarity of a snapshot, the water mushroomed with bright red.

I wondered if that was my brain again, connecting a color to something happening to my body. Maybe the shark had grabbed my arm and my perceptions were exploding.

But I felt no pain.

The red in the water swirled as the shark thrashed.

For a second the red cleared, and I saw that the top of the shark's skull was gone.

It continued to thrash and swirl, and its body bumped against my face. I felt rough sandpaper and saw yellow.

That, I knew, was my brain. Yellow was not a color that belonged here. In a weird way, I found myself noting this new information. My left elbow gave me bright red.

Behind my right knee gave me green. And when something unexpected touched my cheek, yellow.

I didn't think about that for long.

Other, smaller, sharks, drawn by blood, were coming in fast.

The first one, maybe five feet long, lunged in and tore a chunk out of the side of the bull shark. Then another chunk came out. More blood. More sharks.

But if I tried to move past the dying bull shark, I'd attract those same savage bites. I'd become part of the frenzy.

I finally realized I hadn't breathed in about thirty seconds. The top of my snorkel had long been underwater.

As my brain put all of this together, I saw a gaff reach into the water. It was a long-handled pole with a giant hook at the end. We used it to pull fish out of the water.

Now it was dragging the bull shark away from me.

Uncle Gord! Finally! I fought the urge to suck for oxygen as I waited for the shark to be pulled from the now-sideways cage. Once it was clear, Uncle Gord simply let go off the gaff. With a dozen small sharks now ripping at the body of the massive bull shark, it began to sink.

And I was finally free to escape.

chapter twenty

Blackberries again.

It was Friday morning, and I sure didn't want to say good-bye to Key West.

I was standing beside Uncle Gord's old white Chevy truck. Sherri had pulled up on her scooter. As soon as she took off her helmet and shook her long hair free, I tasted the blackberries.

It was going to be a long time before that happened again. Uncle Gord was sending me back to Chicago.

"You sure you like the truck?" he was saying as Sherri walked closer.

"Love it," I lied. In a few places, springs were sticking out of the front seat. The body of the truck had dozens of rust spots from the salty moist air of Key West. Nobody could love a truck like this.

But he and I had been lying to each other since breakfast. Lying is not right, but we had been doing it to protect each other.

And his lie probably had more truth in it than he wanted to admit. He'd said he couldn't afford to keep me or Sherri on as summer workers. He'd said he didn't have enough money to pay what he owed me. Or even to let me stay at his house anymore. He'd offered me the truck instead of my wages.

We both knew it was a lie, because we were both still shaken up about the bull shark. It was a good thing he'd been able to grab his rifle and shoot it. Otherwise yesterday's shark video would have had a much different ending.

I knew he was lying because he was afraid I'd get hurt if I stayed around.

"Hey," Sherri said, "leaving already?"

I didn't trust my voice, so I nodded. I was leaving. I didn't know if Uncle Gord would be all right, but he wasn't letting me stay to help him. I didn't know if Uncle Gord's dive shop would be in business next year, so I didn't know if I'd be back. And that meant I didn't know if I'd see Sherri again.

I'd sure miss the taste of blackberries. But how could I tell her that with Uncle Gord standing right beside the truck?

Sherri gave a crooked smile. "Scared of sharks, I guess."

Uncle Gord laughed. It was a forced laugh, like he had been waiting for an excuse to laugh.

"Should have seen him pull his wet suit off after he got back on the *GypSea*," Uncle Gord told Sherri. "He'd filled it with more than water, if you get my drift."

"Ha, ha," I said.

Uncle Gord opened the driver's door for me to get in. He couldn't get rid of me fast enough.

"Well," I said. "I guess this is good-bye."

"You've got plenty of cash for gas and hotels," Uncle Gord said. "And you have my cell number in case anything goes wrong."

"Yes," I said.

Sherri went around to the other side of the truck.

"Stupid shoelace," I heard her say to herself.

She squatted as Uncle Gord kept talking. Even the top of her head, which was all I could see, was distracting.

"Don't drive for more than four hours at a time," he said. "Make sure you stop and stretch. Take naps too."

"Yes," I said. I wanted to be talking to Sherri. Not to him. But really, what was I going to say? *Hey, Sherri, I think you're really cool. I wish I wasn't so weird, then maybe you could like me too.*

"And we'll see you next summer when business picks up again, right?" His lie.

"Right." My lie.

Sherri was in sight again. She wandered back around the other side of the truck. All the way to the front to where I stood at the driver's door.

"See ya," she said. Casual. She stuck out her hand to shake my hand.

"See ya," I said. I shook her hand. I would not have minded a hug. Like say, for about a half hour. "Hope your shoelace stays tied."

What a dumb thing to say.

"See ya," she said again. She let go of my hand.

"See ya," I said again.

And that was it.

I got in the truck. Started it. And drove away.

chapter twenty-one

As I made my way along Flagler Avenue,
I was the slowest driver on the road. At
every traffic light, I wanted to turn around.
First, I knew Uncle Gord was in trouble.
Second, I didn't want my last good-bye
to Sherri to just be a handshake and two
words.

See ya.

I knew what was going to hurt over the
next few hours.

The mile markers.

About a hundred years earlier, a guy named Henry Flagler completed the railroad that linked Key West to Miami. Mile marker zero was at the Key West Post Office. Mile marker one was one mile closer to Miami. And so on, all the way to Florida City, where the markers ended at 127.5 miles.

At the end of every summer, as Uncle Gord drove me to Miami for my flight to Chicago, I'd see the mile markers, knowing the higher the number, the farther away I was from Key West. It was always depressing.

This time promised to be a lot worse.

Hope your shoelace stays tied. See ya.

Those were going to be my last words to her.

My last words. Not the last words of the summer, knowing I would come back. But probably my last words. Because this wasn't like the other times. Uncle Gord wasn't driving me. It wasn't the end of summer. And there wasn't anything to come back to.

I passed the Key West airport, telling myself I should turn around. But Uncle

Gord had made it clear I was not welcome in Key West.

At mile marker four, I passed the entrance to the Key West Golf Club. It made me wish that Uncle Gord did something safe like golfing, instead of looking for pirate treasure. It made me wish that my biggest worry was trying to hit a golf ball.

As I thought about this, the truck's ride became really bumpy.

A little farther down the road, just before reaching the small stretch of open water to Raccoon Key, I realized the back left tire was going flat.

Normally, this would be bad news.

Instead I grinned.

It was a sign: I was being told I shouldn't leave Key West.

I pulled over onto a side street, Key Haven Road, where there was a big parking lot next to a gas station.

Yup. Good news. I couldn't leave Key West. Not until the tire was fixed. How could Uncle Gord blame me for this?

Another idea hit me.

I stepped out of the truck into the Gulf breeze. I opened the hood and pulled a few spark plug wires loose. Then I tucked them in place so it would look like they were connected. Now I could tell Uncle Gord the engine had stopped working too. That would buy me a day or two longer in Key West. At least the weekend. And the guys who called themselves Miami lawyers would be gone at the end of it.

I'd see what I could do between now and then.

I had just shut the hood when I saw a familiar scooter ridden by a familiar person.

Sherri.

I tasted blackberries.

Yup, things were definitely looking better and better.

chapter twenty-two

"Wow," Sherri said, as she pulled up on her scooter beside the truck. "What a coincidence. I was going out to Raccoon Key because I heard about a job. Lucky for you, huh?"

"Lucky," I said. *Very lucky.*

"How about I give you a ride back?" she said. "You can call a towing service or something from town."

"Sure."

She patted the back of her scooter. "It won't be fast. But it should get us there."

I jumped on the back of the scooter. I was afraid to put my arms around her. She grabbed my hands and wrapped my arms around her waist.

"That's better," she said. "Hold on tight."

Like I wouldn't.

She took us all the way back into downtown Key West. She went slowly, and it was the best half hour of my life.

She parked in front of an ice-cream store.

"Let's talk," she said, pulling off her helmet and shaking her hair loose.

Like I wouldn't.

I bought her a milkshake. Chocolate. Vanilla for me. We sat in the shade of a palmetto.

"Yesterday afternoon," she said after a long slurp, "when you guys were out in the *GypSea*, I came back to the office. I saw Judd inside. I thought it was weird. You know, because of his social security number being wrong. So I watched through the window. He was on the computer. So I know he's up to something."

"Maybe," I said. "But what?" I still didn't know if I should tell her about the three-hundred-million-dollar treasure.

"And don't you think it's weird that you nearly died twice in accidents in one week? I'm sure that's why Gord is sending you away."

"Maybe it's weird," I said again. "Or maybe it's just bad luck." I kept my eyes on my milkshake. She was very distracting, and I didn't want her to know it.

"And one other thing," she said. "Just shaking hands good-bye is rotten."

I lifted my eyes and stared straight into hers.

"Huh?" I managed to say.

"We've been working together for four summers. Maybe you aren't going to be back next summer. Don't you think after all that time it should be a little more than a handshake for good-bye?"

"Um, yes."

"But with Gord there, what could I say to you? I'm glad we can at least have a milk-shake together before you go."

"Me too." I said. I lifted my milkshake as if I were toasting her.

She kept staring at me.

"What?" I said.

"How can you be so stupid?"

"What?"

"I'm not going to throw myself at you," she said. "So you'd better figure out what to say next if you want me to stick around to finish my milkshake."

I nearly choked. *Did she mean...*

"I mean," she said. "There's a reason I don't have a boyfriend. And lots of guys ask me out."

Did she mean...

"And maybe that reason is you," she said.

Wow. I didn't know what to say.

She waited a few moments. Then she frowned at me. And stood up.

"Good-bye then," she said. "I guess I've made a big enough fool out of myself."

"Um, no," I blurted. "Let me explain."

She sat down. "Okay. You've got thirty seconds to give me a reason to stay."

"I'm too weird for someone like you," I said.

"You don't seem too weird. And I've known you a long time."

"Your face. Each time I see it, I taste blackberries."

She raised an eyebrow. Puzzled.

I took a deep breath. And explained.

chapter twenty-three

I spent the rest of the day looking for Judd Warner. I finally saw him leaving the dock in the late afternoon.

It was easy to stay out of sight. It was a Friday evening. Lots of people on the streets.

I followed him back to Uncle Gord's dive shop. That shouldn't have been surprising. After all, Judd Warner—if that was his name—worked for Uncle Gord.

It wasn't surprising, either, that the dive shop was empty. With me and Sherri out of work, only Judd and Uncle Gord still worked there. And I knew Uncle Gord was getting ready for another night trip on the *GypSea*.

What was surprising was that Judd broke into Uncle Gord's office.

I was watching from a window near the back of the shop.

Judd snooped around for a few minutes, and when he stepped outside the office again, he had a pistol in his hand.

I crouched farther down behind the window. I waited for him to walk past. I held my breath and hoped he couldn't hear how loud my heart was beating.

Judd stepped past the counter. He didn't look behind him. He didn't see me.

He was wearing black pants and a black T-shirt. As he walked toward the back room, he folded a piece of paper and stuck it in his back pocket. He lifted his shirt and put his pistol into his belt. He dropped the shirt to cover the pistol.

I kept holding my breath. I watched his shadow. It took a step toward the front, then was gone. He stepped outside. A few moments later, the door at the front opened and closed. I heard the turn of the key. Judd had locked the front door behind him.

I stood up.

What should I do?

If I called the police, what would I tell them? It didn't look like Judd had robbed Uncle Gord. It seemed like the piece of paper had been important. The police would ask me what was missing, and I wouldn't be able to tell them. Plus, it would be Judd's word against mine.

I wanted to let Uncle Gord know about this. But then I'd have to tell him I had not left Key West.

I stood for a while longer. Flies buzzed against the window. Other than that and the street noises, the dive shop was very quiet.

I thought it was strange that Judd was wearing black jeans and a black T-shirt. Although it was early evening, it was still very hot. Why wear black in this heat? I had never seen Judd wearing black before.

I grinned at how smart I was. If you were going to follow people at night, wouldn't you wear something dark?

It was Friday night. Judd knew that Uncle Gord would be going out in the dive boat tonight. Judd was probably going to follow them. Maybe even go on board the dive boat. There was plenty of room to hide on it.

There were two ways to find out if I was right.

I could tell Uncle Gord. He and his three friends from Miami, whoever they were, could watch for Judd. But if they stopped him, it would be easy for Judd to come up with an excuse for being near the dive boat. Worse, if I was wrong about Judd, I'd look stupid.

Or I could keep my mouth shut and follow Judd myself. If he really was doing something wrong, I'd know it by watching him. I'd already waited behind the dive shop too long to know where he had gone. How could I catch up to him?

I slapped my forehead. If Judd was going to spy on Uncle Gord tonight, there was only one place Judd would go. To the *GypSea*.

The sun was almost ready to set. It wouldn't be too long before Uncle Gord and his friends would be on the dive boat, getting ready to leave. If Judd was following them, he'd be there too.

But I still had a little time. I ran to the beach house that Uncle Gord rented. My stuff was still in a suitcase in the truck. But I'd be able to fit into Uncle Gord's clothes. All I needed to do was find dark clothes.

Then I would be ready to hunt the hunter.

chapter twenty-four

I reached the docks just before sunset. I had on a dark summer jacket and a pair of dark track pants.

I stood still and looked around. The smell of salt water filled the air. Pelicans stood on the dock posts. There were dozens of boats tied to the long dock. A lot of people were walking around. None of them were Judd or Uncle Gord or his friends from Miami.

Past the docks, the sun had almost dropped to the place where ocean met sky.

It was orange, a postcard kind of sunset. In less than half an hour, most of the light would be gone.

I already knew where I would wait and watch. I carried a gym bag in one hand. I had a fishing pole in my other hand. I had a ballcap pulled low over my eyes. I was going to sit at the end of the dock, where I could keep an eye on the *GypSea*.

It was the fourth boat down, bobbing in the wake of passing boats.

I walked onto the dock. The *GypSea* was empty as I passed it. Fifty yards down, I reached the end of the dock. I sat and dropped a fishing line into the water. I held the fishing pole as if I was waiting for a fish to take the bait. With a slight turn of my head, I kept an eye on the *GypSea*. Most of my face was hidden by my ballcap.

Ten minutes later, Judd Warner walked onto the dock.

I ducked my head down even more. I didn't think he would give me a second look, not if he was worried about getting onto Uncle Gord's boat.

He hopped onto the *GypSea* as if he owned it. A second later, he had moved into the front of the boat. It was a big boat. There were a lot of places he could hide. A few seconds later, he was out of sight.

My heart began to race. I had guessed right!

I waited a few more minutes. Once Judd was hidden, he wouldn't be able to see me get on the boat. As I waited, I went over my plan again. At this point, I could change my mind. I could wait for Uncle Gord and his friends to get to the boat. I could tell them about Judd. They could find him.

But then they would never know what he really meant to do. No, I told myself, the best way was to wait to see what Judd wanted. I would stick to my plan.

I stood and picked up the gym bag. I walked down to the *GypSea*. Front to back, it was sixty feet long. More than twenty good-sized steps. It had a couple of cabins beneath the top deck. Judd was hiding in there somewhere.

I stepped onto the boat as lightly as I could. I didn't want him to hear me or feel the boat rock.

The sun had dropped out of sight, and the last rays of light made long shadows on the deck. I knew of a place where no one would see me when it was light out. It would be that much safer at night. I tiptoed to my hiding spot.

It was a wide upright locker where we stored wet suits that we rented to divers. I pulled it open, moved inside and pushed myself among the wet suits. They smelled of salt water.

There was just enough room inside for me to set my gym bag at my feet. I reached out for the door and closed it almost all the way, leaving a few inches to give me a crack to see out.

Then I reached down to my gym bag again. I pulled out a speargun.

After all, Judd had a pistol. I needed to be armed too.

chapter twenty-five

At nine o'clock, it was completely dark.
I heard voices as Uncle Gord and his friends
stepped onto the boat. I heard clanking as
they set down their scuba tanks and the
rest of their gear.

I didn't need to see them to know
what they looked like. I had seen them a
couple of other times. All three looked like
football players. They had short hair and
square faces. I remembered seeing them

and thinking lawyers like that would be good for scaring judges.

I wasn't worried that they might open the locker I was hiding in. They wouldn't need any of the rental wet suits. All of them had their own wet suits. People who dive a lot don't like using rental wet suits. Why? It sounds gross, but there are no toilets underwater. Sometimes divers have to go so bad, they go in their wet suits and let the water wash it away.

The four of them moved around the boat. They didn't talk much. There were other sounds: the slapping of water against the boat; laughter from parties on other boats. But on Uncle Gord's boat, all I could hear was my own breathing.

Then I heard Uncle Gord's footsteps as he walked to the controls. He started the engine blowers. Boat engines are beneath the deck. Air doesn't move much under there. If there are any gasoline fumes around the engines, the fumes could explode when the engines start.

A blower fans the old air out to make it safe.

A few minutes later, Uncle Gord started both engines. They roared as he gave them gas. Once they were warm, he let them drop to a steady chug. He yelled out instructions to the three guys to untie the ropes that held the boat to the dock.

Then he backed the boat from the dock. He turned it and slowly pulled out of the marina. The boat rocked a little in the smooth water.

It took a few minutes to get to open water. Finally, he was able to give the engines some gas and take the boat to full speed. It bounced harder against the waves. The wet suits slapped me as the boat moved up and down.

Uncle Gord ran the engines hard for another twenty minutes. Then he shut them down, and the boat slowed to a stop.

I heard clanking. Uncle Gord had hit the switch to drop the anchor. There was a small motor that unwound the anchor chain. The motor whined, and the chain clanked as the anchor fell through the water. I counted the seconds. When the clanking stopped, I guessed we were in about eighty feet of water.

Through the crack of the open door, I saw the beams of flashlights as they got their equipment ready. I wondered why Uncle Gord didn't turn on any lights to help them.

Then I noticed I didn't see any of the small running lights that were supposed to let other boaters know where we were. In a way, it was unsafe. But in another way, no problem. As long as they were alert to the lights of other craft on the water, they could stay invisible and avoid a collision.

At first, though, even this small risk seemed strange. Uncle Gord always does things the safe way.

Then I figured it out. They were here to look for three hundred million dollars in pirates' gold. They had spent every weekend searching in secret. They didn't *want* anyone to know where they were. So why should this weekend be any different?

But it was.

Two people were on board the boat who didn't belong there.

chapter twenty-six

I nearly fell asleep. I was standing in the locker, but the wet suits pressing against me kept me from falling. Nothing had happened for at least an hour.

It was weird. None of them had even gone into the water yet. The boat just sat in darkness. The four of them just sat without talking. If this was a search for treasure, why weren't they underwater?

Were the four of them waiting? If so, for what?

Judd Warner had been just as quiet as the rest of us. Wherever he was hidden, he was deciding to wait too.

I nodded off. My face hit a wet suit. It woke me.

I heard the faint sound of another engine.

A boat?

A few minutes later, I decided it was an airplane.

The sound grew louder.

I decided to risk poking my head out of the locker.

Suddenly, the boat's lights flashed on.

Then off.

Then on.

Then off. This time, the lights stayed off.

The airplane passed over us low and loud. It kept going.

I didn't get it. What had just happened?

Whatever it was, it meant action. When I heard scrapes of movement on the deck, I pulled my head back into the locker. Good thing. The three lawyers from Miami were moving around to get geared up. One of them passed so close to the locker I heard his breathing through the crack in the open door.

Then they were gone again. I heard splashing. One splash. Two splashes. Three. They had all just entered the water.

I pushed open the locker door just enough to see the dark shadow of Uncle Gord standing at the edge of the boat. Far away were the faint lights of the shoreline.

What was happening?

I opened the door a little further. Uncle Gord had his back to me and was looking out over the water. I tried to see past him to figure out what he was waiting for.

I saw another dark shadow move quietly behind Uncle Gord.

Judd Warner! With his pistol pointed at Uncle Gord.

I slowly pushed open the locker door.

It was all in front of me. The deck of the boat. Judd Warner standing behind Uncle Gord. Uncle Gord looking into the water. And the black, black ocean beyond.

"Hands behind your back," Judd said in a low voice.

Uncle Gord started to move.

Judd stepped forward and pressed his pistol against Uncle Gord's back.

"Hands behind your back or I pull the trigger."

Slowly, Uncle Gord put his hands behind him.

Slowly, I stepped out of the locker. With the loaded speargun in my hand.

"Good," Judd Warner said to Uncle Gord. "It's a lot easier taking you before those three gorillas get back on the boat."

I heard a click. Judd Warner had just handcuffed Uncle Gord's wrists together.

I raised my speargun. The safety was still on, but Judd didn't have to know that. I was afraid I might trigger the spear by accident.

"Drop your gun," I said in a shaky voice. "I've got a speargun, and I'll shoot if I have to."

chapter twenty-seven

"You don't know what you're doing, Ian," Judd said. "You're making a mistake."

"I'm going to count to three. Then I shoot. One...two..."

Judd bent over and set the gun on the deck.

"Now unlock the handcuffs," I said.

"If you'll listen to me," Judd said. "You would know that—"

"One...two..."

Judd reached into his pocket. I watched carefully to make sure he wasn't going for a knife. A few seconds later, he unlocked Uncle Gord.

Uncle Gord turned around.

"Ian?"

"I followed him," I explained. "I didn't want to tell you until I knew what was happening."

"I owe you one," Uncle Gord said. "Keep him covered while I get the gun."

I pointed the speargun at Judd's chest. Judd kept still. I couldn't see his face in the dark. Just the outline of his body.

When Uncle Gord had the pistol in his hand, he handcuffed Judd Warner and put the key in his pocket.

"We can relax now, Ian," Uncle Gord said, stepping away from Judd. "This guy won't be able to do anything to us."

"What is all of this about?" I asked. "It doesn't look like a treasure hunt."

"You're smart, Ian," Uncle Gord said. "That's what I've always liked about you."

Uncle Gord was backing away from Judd as he spoke. He kept the pistol pointed at Judd as he moved beside me.

"You want to know what this is about?" Uncle Gord said.

"Yeah," I said. "All of this is weird. And what is Judd doing?"

"I'll tell you in a second," Uncle Gord said. He turned to me and in a single movement pressed the pistol against my head. "First, I want you to throw the speargun overboard."

"Huh?"

"I'm not joking. Throw your speargun into the water behind you. Or I'll put a neat little hole into your head."

I was frozen with disbelief.

I heard the pistol click as Uncle Gord brought the hammer back.

I threw the speargun behind me. It splashed into the darkness a second later.

"See," Uncle Gord said. "You are smart. Now stand beside Judd where I can watch both of you."

This wasn't real, I told myself. It felt like I was walking through waist-deep glue as I moved to stand beside Judd.

"Look behind you," Uncle Gord said. "That's your answer."

At first, I saw nothing but black. It hurt my eyes, I was looking so hard. Finally, I thought I saw something. For a moment, I wondered if it was my imagination. It seemed like a speck of light on the water.

A few seconds later, I knew my eyes were not playing tricks on me. The speck of light glowed brighter and brighter. It was heading right toward the boat.

Then, in a flash, I put it all together. The boat sitting in the dark for an hour. Waiting for an airplane to pass overhead. Lights flashing to let the airplane know the boat was there. Something in the water, marked by a glowing light.

I didn't want to believe it, but it couldn't be anything else. It was a safe guess that Uncle Gord wasn't searching for treasure on his Friday and Saturday nights.

Instead it could only be one thing.

Drugs.

chapter twenty-eight

I knew a little about it. A person can't spend much time in Florida without knowing that smuggling and dealing drugs is big business. Florida has the wide-open ocean. It was the perfect place to move drugs into the United States. It's against the law, of course. But that doesn't stop people. Drugs mean big money.

My Uncle Gord. A drug dealer? Maybe pretending his business was failing so no one suspected what he was doing?

I wanted to kick myself for not seeing this earlier. For believing his three friends were lawyers. Guys who were built like football players. These were the kind of guys you wanted around if you were breaking the law. These were the kind of guys you wanted around if you were working with dope dealers who didn't care if they murdered to make their money.

Thinking about it, I saw his plan was perfect. First, he told people they were spearfishing at night. It was easy to believe that's why they went out on weekends. After all, Uncle Gord ran a scuba-diving business for a living.

Then, to make sure people really were fooled, he probably started the rumors about a treasure hunt himself. It was like a lie within a lie. No one would ever guess there was a third lie within the second lie. And then the fourth lie: that his business was broke. Nobody in Florida who was a drug dealer ever looked broke. A bunch of perfect lies.

"You use this boat for a pickup, don't you?" I said to Uncle Gord. "You make it look like business has been bad, and you're making extra money by coming out here to pick up drugs dropped from an airplane. Those three guys went into the water to get it."

"You're almost right," Uncle Gord said. "We're anchored on the edge of the strong part of the Gulf Stream. Whatever drops from the plane will pass close to this boat. And yes, the three men are out there to look for it and pick it up."

Splashing noises reached us. They were close to the boat now. I took a quick peek. The light bobbed in the water. I couldn't see much around it except the heads and shoulders of the scuba divers.

"Boys," Uncle Gord called out to them. "Come in real easy. We've got company. Nothing for you to worry about, but I didn't want you surprised."

"The FBI clown?" one of the voices called up to the boat.

FBI?

"Yup," Uncle Gord said.

"How do we know he isn't holding a gun to your head?" one of the other voices asked.

Uncle Gord stepped over to the control panels of the boat. He flicked on a light. It showed him clearly. His gray hair. His bushy mustache. The gun in his hand. And the cold, cold look in his eyes.

Uncle Gord snapped the light off again. "You saw enough to know I'm in charge?"

"We're coming aboard," came the answer.

There were more splashing sounds.

One man stepped onto the deck near us, dripping water from his wet suit. A second man. And a third. All big. Very big.

What surprised me was the fourth man. Much shorter than the other three. Where had he come from?

"What is going on?" the short man asked in an angry voice. He had a strong Spanish accent. "FBI? This was not part of our agreement."

chapter twenty-nine

"Yes, Ian," Uncle Gord said. "If it makes you feel better, I'm not into drugs."

I wasn't sure anything could make me feel better. Judd was an FBI agent and I'd put him in danger. My uncle was pointing a gun at me. Three big guys were behind him to help. And a fourth guy had come out of nowhere.

"Enough talk," one of the big guys said.

"What difference does it make?" Uncle Gord said. "I've got the gun. They're not going anywhere. And this is our last run anyway."

To me, Uncle Gord said, "Cubans. That's what we do. Help Cubans make it into the United States. We help them become citizens. We help them leave behind a terrible life."

"Don't buy into that," Judd Warner said. Coming out of the darkness beside me, his voice surprised me.

"Oh, really," Uncle Gord told Judd. "If you're so smart, you tell Ian."

"Not many Cubans can afford your uncle," Judd said to me. "The man standing in front of us is a wanted criminal. He got his money by dealing drugs in Cuba."

"Shoot this man!" the short Cuban shouted.

"Not yet," Uncle Gord said. "I want to hear more."

Judd didn't say anything.

Uncle Gord pointed his gun at my chest. "Tell us what you know, Mr. FBI, or this kid dies."

"I know it was me you were trying to kill with the broken valve on the scuba tank," Judd said.

"Yes," Uncle Gord said. "We've been onto you for a least a week. Ever since that letter came from the IRS saying your identification was phony."

Judd frowned. "What?"

Uncle Gord ignored the question. "Plus you asked a few too many questions. We did want you dead before tonight, but it had to look like an accident. Too bad the wrong guy went down."

"*You* wrecked the tank?" I said to Uncle Gord. "But, but..."

"Sorry," he said. It didn't sound like he meant it. "That's the way it goes."

Sorry? All he said was *sorry?* This was my uncle. My sister's brother. The guy I had been visiting nearly every summer I could remember.

"Keep going," Uncle Gord said to Judd. "What else do you know?"

The boat bobbed gently in the waves. A nice warm breeze crossed my face. Just a regular Florida night. It seemed unreal to be watching my uncle with a gun in his hand.

"It's a simple way of doing it," Judd said. "You've got a pilot in a seaplane who picks them up from a rowboat off the coast of Cuba. You know that airplanes are watched on radar and that it's too risky to bring them into Florida that way. So the plane drops them into the water, and you pick them up. You hide them on the boat and bring them in. You have fake passports ready for them and you send them on their way."

"A hundred thousand dollars," Uncle Gord said. "Cash. Divide it four ways. That's twenty-five grand for each of us every Friday and Saturday night."

He shook his head sadly. "It was a great way to make money. Too bad it ends tonight. You work for the FBI. I'm sure you've been filing reports. Even after you're dead, we'll have trouble. So we decided this run is our last."

After you're dead? My uncle was going to kill a man?

"And by the way, Ian," Uncle Gord said. "We'll have to kill you too."

chapter thirty

"After we drop the Cuban off at Key West, we're going to the Bahamas anyway," Uncle Gord said to the men behind him. "So on our way east, we might as well put weights on these two and let them go off the wall. That way, no one will ever find their bodies."

I felt my knees go weak.

Off the wall.

Uncle Gord was talking about the continental shelf. For about the first three miles from shore, the ocean didn't get much deeper than 150 feet. The land beneath the water was like a shelf.

But three miles out, the land just dropped away. It was like stepping off the edge of a table. Divers called it going off the wall. The ocean went from 150 feet deep to 10,000 feet. Nearly two miles straight down into deep, deep blackness.

"Good idea," one of the men said. "No bodies, no more trouble."

Uncle Gord handed the pistol to the closest man. "Cover me," Uncle Gord said. "I'm going to handcuff them together. If one of them even blinks, shoot."

Uncle Gord dug the handcuff key out of his pocket. He unsnapped the cuffs. Then he cuffed Judd's left hand to my right hand.

"Keep covering them," Uncle Gord said. "One of you get behind the wheel. Take the boat in so we can drop off the Cuban."

As the boat began moving again, Uncle Gord wired a length of anchor chain to the middle of the handcuffs. The other end of the chain was attached to the anchor.

I kept hoping that Judd would do something to save us. I mean, he was an FBI undercover agent. Didn't he have some kind of training?

But there was a pistol pointed at us. Judd didn't try anything.

"How could you do this?" I said.

Uncle Gord shrugged. "Twice a week since the beginning of May. Do the math. I'm nearly a million dollars richer. I'm not going to jail, not when I'm that rich. And I can't trust you to keep your mouth shut."

"But I'm your nephew."

He shrugged and taped my mouth so we couldn't yell for help when we got to Key West.

The boat reached the docks. They kept us out of sight. They dropped the Cuban off and headed back out in the darkness.

Toward the deep, deep water. Where they were going to drop us off the wall.

chapter thirty-one

I guess the worst way to die is to see it coming. If you're in a car accident or something like that, you don't have time to worry.

Instead I was on a boat going thirty miles an hour, knowing that in less than ten miles I would be thrown overboard. There was hardly any time left, but there was also way too much time to think.

I thought of everything nice I would miss. Orange sunsets. The feel of sand on bare feet, of sun on skin.

Milkshakes with Sherri.

Then I thought of how my dad had left me.

I thought of how my uncle had betrayed me too.

I thought of how Sherri had said she wanted me to be her guy.

I cried. Not sobbing crying, like a baby. But tears of sadness that the wind pushed across my face.

I was scared.

When the *GypSea* stopped, it took all four of them to get us into the water. Uncle Gord and the three big ugly guys.

One of them lifted me. One of them lifted Judd. And two of them lifted the anchor that was hooked to the middle of the handcuffs that held Judd and me together.

I couldn't yell at them. My mouth was still taped shut.

Even though I had one hand free and one hand attached to the handcuff that was wired to the anchor, I didn't try anything.

I had given up. What chance did I have? It was two miles straight down in the black water. If the anchor was so heavy it took two guys to lift, it was going to pull me and Judd down like a piano falling through air.

Judd didn't fight either. We were just a couple of sacks of potatoes.

"We'll toss them on the count of three," Uncle Gord said.

"One..."

They swung once.

"Two..."

A bigger swing.

"Three!"

They let go on the third upswing. We cleared the edge of the boat and dropped through the air.

I drew one final breath through my nostrils.

Then...

Splash. Just one sound. Judd and the anchor and I hit the water at the same time.

The water was cold. We dropped in total black silence.

chapter thirty-two

We fell and fell and fell. We sank so fast
that the water peeled my shirt and pants
upward.

And still we fell into the deep black.

My lungs began to hurt. Any second I
wouldn't be able to help myself. I would
suck for air through my nose. All I would get
would be water. I would be dead long before
we hit the ocean floor two miles down.

Then, suddenly, the water stopped
tugging at me.

I was free!

Both my arms could move!

My lungs were screaming for air. I bit down hard and kicked my legs.

Up, up, I told myself, kick up!

I fought against the water. I had to get to the surface. All I could think of was reaching air.

I kicked. But the harder I kicked, the more I needed air.

I kicked. I felt myself growing weaker, but still I kicked.

And I reached cool air. The black of the water was now the black of night. With stars above. I tried to gasp for air, but my mouth was taped. I got a little air through my nostrils, but I needed more. I ripped the tape from my mouth and pulled in lungful after lungful of air.

The noise of the *GypSea* grew fainter and fainter as it left me behind.

I took in more air. It was great to be alive.

It hit me. *I was alive.* What had happened? Where was Judd?

There was a splash beside me.

"Judd?" I called out.

"Over here." His voice croaked just like mine.

We kept splashing until we were side by side. We dog-paddled to keep our heads above the water.

"I can't believe this," I said. "How did you do that?"

He coughed out water. "I had the key in my free hand."

He stopped again to cough out more water. "I didn't dare try to unlock the handcuffs until we were in the water. I had to unlock your side first, because if I didn't, you'd still be dropping and I'd have no way to catch you..."

"Um, thanks," I said.

"Don't thank me yet," he said. "We're miles from shore. I'm not a good swimmer. And I'm scared of sharks."

"Let me show you something," I said. "You got us here. I'll get you to land."

chapter thirty-three

He was paddling hard. He was afraid.

"Listen," I said. "Slow it down. It doesn't take much effort to paddle. And if you swim in jerky movements, you draw in sharks. They look for quick, hard movements. It makes them think of scared or hurt fish. And that makes them think of food."

"I hate this," Judd said. "Thinking of sharks circling us."

I did too. I had strong memories of watching the bull shark close in on me. But it wouldn't do to add to Judd's fear. So I didn't say anything about it.

Instead I got him thinking about doing something positive.

"You can float without moving much," I said. "Take a big breath. It will fill your lungs with air and help you float. When you breathe out, you paddle a bit to keep your head above the water. Then breathe in again."

"Thanks for the lesson," he said.

"No problem," I said. "We may be in the water for hours.

Without warning, a blinking light appeared on the surface of the water. It was so strange, it took me a second to identify it. Emergency light. On a...

"It's a life jacket," Judd said. "Must be from the *GypSea*. Look around. I'll bet we find another."

"But why?" This didn't make sense.

"Trust me," he said. "If there's one, there should be two."

I couldn't believe it. It only took thirty seconds for us to find it. And about another ten seconds for me to slip it on.

"Much easier than paddling," I said. He probably couldn't see my grin in the dark. But I didn't grin for long. There was something else to worry about. "Don't move your legs. Sharks won't have a clue we're here."

I couldn't stop thinking about how weird it was to find these life jackets.

I mentioned this to Judd.

"I don't think it's weird at all," he said. "No weirder than having a handcuff key in my free hand."

"It wasn't a spare or something?"

"No," he said. "Let me tell you something about your Uncle Gord."

I felt my jaws clench. "You mean the guy who tried to kill us?"

"The guy who saved our lives." Judd bobbed, speaking quietly. "You don't really think he meant what he said about getting rid of you, do you?"

I was silent.

"Look," Judd said. "I was brought in undercover to investigate some loan sharking. If you think real sharks are vicious, they're nothing compared to the human sharks who lend desperate people money."

I stared at the stars. "Uncle Gord was having trouble with his business."

"He couldn't get money from the bank. He was at his maximum credit limit. So some guys in Miami lent it to him. At a huge interest rate that he couldn't repay. It's illegal, but it happens all the time."

"That's why the FBI is involved," I said.

"When they had a good squeeze on him, they forced him to help out with smuggling other Cuban criminals into the United States. I needed to prove it."

"You said he didn't want to kill me." I really wanted to believe this.

"Didn't he try to send you out of town?"

"Yeah," I said.

"I'm pretty sure he acted tough in front of them so they'd believe he didn't care about you. But as he wired us to the anchor, he slipped me the key."

"What?" I grinned.

"Sure," Judd said. "And he must have tossed out the life jackets without them seeing it."

I felt like crying again. From relief. Because worse than dying was thinking that someone I'd trusted had betrayed me.

"You don't know how much better that makes me feel," I said into the darkness to Judd.

"Probably as good as I'll feel if a ship or an airplane sees us. It's going to be a long night, even in life jackets."

chapter thirty-four

It must have been my relief at being alive.
Or sharing what we'd gone through. But in
the darkness, I felt the need to talk.

"Judd, have you heard of something
called synesthesia?"

"No," he said.

"It means joined perception."

He repeated it. "Joined perception."

"Yeah. I've got it. For a long time I
thought I was crazy. Now I just know I'm
strange."

"Synesthesia."

I did my best to explain. But for people who don't have it—and that's nearly everybody—it's almost impossible to explain. It's almost like trying to explain what color is. Nobody can really explain it. Partly because the brain is so difficult to explain.

At least I knew I wasn't crazy.

Only different.

And after keeping it secret from everyone my whole life, I'd just confessed it twice in one day.

First to Sherri.

Now to Judd. Maybe because Sherri hadn't treated me like Frankenstein when she found out.

When I finished, Judd said, "You're a lucky kid, Ian Hill."

"Lucky?"

"Your Uncle Gord risked his life to save yours. If those guys had caught on to what he was doing, he would have been tied to the anchor with us. You're pretty lucky to have someone who cares about you like he does."

Judd continued. "And to be able to see colors when you feel something? That's lucky too. You get to experience the world in a cool way. I hope you'll always remember that."

I had to admit, hearing it come from him did make me feel lucky. Because that's exactly what Sherri had said when I told her. *Cool.*

I was trying to think of something to say to that when I heard what sounded like an engine.

I froze.

Maybe the Miami guys on Uncle Gord's boat had discovered the missing life jackets and turned around to finish the job.

Then I realized the sound was coming from the air.

"Hey!" I said to Judd. "Look at those lights."

It was a helicopter. Coming in low and fast. Straight toward us.

It passed over us.

We yelled, even knowing there was no way that a pilot could hear us.

But it turned around and circled us a couple of times. Then it hovered above us, pinpointing us by our blinking life-jacket lights.

Five minutes later, we were safe inside the chopper.

Headed home.

chapter thirty-five

It wasn't luck that the chopper found us.

With the life jackets, Uncle Gord had also thrown a search-and-rescue radar transponder into the Gulf waters. It was a small orange tube that floated and sent out emergency signals to the marine-rescue radio band.

Yes, he'd taken care of us.

And, as it turned out, he'd done more than that. He'd left a lot of information for the FBI on his computer, something they discovered when they used a search warrant to go through everything he owned. It gave details of all the men he'd rescued. Judd told me later that Uncle Gord's information gave them a good chance of finding all the illegal Cubans.

As for Uncle Gord, he totally disappeared. Except for the postcard I got about two weeks later. From Jamaica.

All it said was: *Made it. Glad you did too. I'll be back when I can.*

He must have contacted someone in Key West to find out I'd survived. His postcard meant a lot to me. Uncle Gord really was like a dad to me. One who bothered to let me know he was alive. And one who made sure I knew I'd see him again.

I told most of this to Sherri one morning about ten days later. All of it except for the bit about the postcard. It would be a lot better if the world thought there was no way of finding Uncle Gord.

But there was one last mystery.

I solved that one too, the morning I spoke to Sherri.

"You're going back in a few days," she said.

We were having the same milkshakes under the same tree.

"But I've decided something," I said. "When I finish high school next year, I'm coming back to stay."

"You like Key West that much?"

"It gets in your blood," I said. "I couldn't think of living anywhere else."

"So you like Key West that much." She glared at me.

"Yup." I grinned. I knew what she was wanting me to say. "Plus I do like a certain girl who lives here too."

She grinned back. "I guess that pebble really paid off."

I frowned at her. "Pebble?"

"Sure. Remember the morning you were getting ready to leave? When Gord was giving you all those instructions about how to drive back to Chicago? When I pretended my shoelace was untied?"

Now I nodded.

"While he was talking to you, I went to the rear left tire. I unscrewed the cap. I put a tiny pebble on the valve stem. And screwed the cap back on so the tire would leak."

It took me a second. "The flat tire wasn't an accident?"

"Not a chance," she said. "And I was following you on my scooter to be able to give you a ride back."

She reached across and touched my cheek with the back of her fingers.

As I felt the softness of her fingers across my skin, I saw a burst of yellow.

And loved it.

Author's Notes

Synesthesia

The condition that Ian experiences in this story is rare but real. There are people who feel, taste and hear color. Synesthesia is a neural condition in which two or more senses intertwine. To scientists, however, the cause is still a mystery. Some wonder if we all experience this as infants, before our brains learn to separate the senses, so that when we are very young, we not only hear our mother's voice, but see it and smell it too.

The Vandenberg

The sinking of the *Vandenberg* to form an artificial reef off Key West has been delayed, perhaps indefinitely. This project, if accomplished, is meant to provide marine habitat and a major diving attraction.

To track the project's progress, go to www.bigshipwrecks.com.

Mel Fisher and the Atocha *Mother Lode*

Mel Fisher was a famous American treasure hunter who established a museum in Key West. On July 20, 1985, he discovered the wreck of the Spanish galleon *Nuestra Señora de Atocha* off the Florida Keys. It included forty tons of gold and silver, and about 100,000 Spanish silver coins, known as "pieces of eight," plus emeralds and 1,000 silver bars. Altogether, this find was worth an estimated $450 million.

To learn more about this discovery, visit www.melfisher.org/1622.htm.

Sigmund Brouwer is the best-selling author of many books for children and young adults. He has contributed to the Orca Currents series (*Sewer Rats*, *Wired*) and the Orca Sports series (*Blazer Drive*, *All-Star Pride*, *Chief Honor*, *Rebel Glory*, *Scarlet Thunder*, *Tiger Threat*, *Titan Clash*, *Cobra Strike*, *Winter Hawk Star*, *Hitmen Triumph* and *Hurricane Power*). Sigmund enjoys visiting schools to talk about his books. Interested teachers can find out more by e-mailing authorbookings@coolreading.com.

Titles in the Series

orca sports